# A Battleaxe and a Metal Arm 8:

## *Path of the Forgotten*

Samuel Fleming

ii

Copyright © 2021 by Samuel Fleming

All rights reserved. No part of this book may be reproduced or used in any manner without written permission of the copyright owner except for the use of quotations in a book review.

Cover Art by David Leahey

ISBN-13: 978-1-954679-21-4 (paperback)
ISBN-13: 978-1-954679-20-7 (ebook)

Thank you to my Beta Readers

and to my First Reader,

Mel.

iv

# Contents

"I would rather be the soul
taken early—the soul
struggling to stay—than the
one forever denied that
eternal rest.
—unknown

# Previously...

Helesys and Taunauk's journey through the realms took them outside of the confines of the dungeon and to a vast beach. Sand dunes and shoreline stretched out as far as they could see. They walked toward the one blemish on the sight—toward a castle crumbling in the distance.

They passed a living mass of seaweed that feasted on gulls—a grisly cycle in which the seagulls were kept alive as long as possible, so that they didn't die and disappear from the realm. It was a grotesque sight and one that they would witness again in the realm.

The crumbling castle in the distance was half-buried in sand, and occupied by two solitary men. The pair lived in squalor in the castle, their meager lives punctuated by the magic of an old shield—on every third day, the pair would surf the waves, using the magic of the shield to aid them.

Farther down the beach, Helesys and Taunauk came to the beached ship, the *Malorienta*, and her crew in the process of repairing it. It was there that they encountered their comrade, Shawn. Together, the three heroes helped with the final repairs and loading of the ship, and resolved to set sail with Captain Besting and the crew.

But the waters of the endless sea were perilous beyond compare. Before they even left the shallows, they were set upon by a giant crab, so large that it was covered in rock and coral, and had arms made of water elementals. Taunauk, Shawn, and the capable fighters repelled the watery arms, while Helesys blasted away the massive claws. In the end, Helesys called upon the power of the Ring of Winter to freeze the sea between the monster and the ship, giving the *Malorienta* just enough time to slip away unscathed.

Farther out to sea, they found small islands dotted by more horror. Dozens of Terrans appeared on the beaches—Terran in shape only—and began to lure the *Malorienta* with siren songs. Helesys and Shawn were among two of the only ones unaffected, and so they took action. Shawn ran to the helm to steer the ship away. Helesys tried to counterspell the creatures, but their sheer numbers proved to be too much, and she was forced to use her holding magic on the crew. Heavy-handed as she was, her spell worked and held the crew still… even the ones that had already leapt overboard and were drowning beneath the waves. The death of most of the crew were averted, but at a cost not all would forgive.

The *Malorienta* did not stop—not until they reached the Narrows. The great cliffs rose higher even than the Infinite Wall. Captain Besting admitted that he would rather not stop, but the dangerous passage through the cliffs would be impassable in darkness. That night he revealed that they had never made it through… that he and the crew had sailed and perished many times aboard the ship, that were bound to the *Malorienta* in life and in death. And that night he shared why he preferred not to anchor in the surrounding waters. Man-eating eels came up from the depths under the cover of darkness.

In preparation, the crew barricaded themselves below in the hold. It was there that they stumbled upon Pitiful Lull. Both the creature and Captain Besting explained that particular Lull had been with them for many iterations, and Shawn confirmed in his recent travels through the rusted prison of the fishmen that Pitiful Lull was indeed still there—it seemed that Lull's mind and essence were split across the realms as part of its unfortunate accident.

The eels set upon them moments later—starfish-like creatures with circular mouths. Helesys, Taunauk, and Shawn braced the barricade, but eventually Helesys was forced to open fire through the small openings. Her blasts tore through the creatures. The creatures then started to eat their wounded brethren. The grisly sounds continued long through the night until the creatures left with first light.

At light of day, the *Malorienta* and her crew crossed the narrows. Most sheltered below deck, save for the able-bodied to rig the sails and clear the deck of rocks that would weigh the ship down. Helesys used her gauntlet to blast apart the larger rocks, and with her protection, the ship made it through the perilous passage for the first time.

That night, the crew celebrated. Meanwhile, Helesys remembered great elven ballrooms and Shawn dwelled on the illusion of the dungeon—the false stars, and the lie of the moon and barely risen sun.

The next morning, they awoke to a gargantuan storm that blotted out the sky and rose waves higher even than the cliffs of the Narrows. The *Malorienta* and her crew were drowned in the waves. Helesys's only consolation was the fleeting memory of her mother, Wynbella, and her sister, Aradi—her mother's warmth and her sister's suspicious grin. Helesys remembered cutting her hair to join the elven legion… and that it was only by illusion magic that it still appeared long.

Helesys awoke on the sand—alone. The beach was not the one her and her comrades walked previously. No, it was a space between. The ambiguous voice addressed her by name and the voice came from the air, or from the ether itself. It would not reveal its identity, but beseeched her help to defeat the Wolf-King. There was a powerful artifact deep beneath the endless sea, and that Zhug's treasure horde held the key to reaching the depths: The Machine of Antrikaumora.

Then she awoke again, this time in the starting room of the dungeon, alongside Taunauk. He had been brought to the same beach to have a similar conversation. He asked the voice why it was they specifically who had been chosen, gifted with the power to bring back items and artifacts after death. And it had given the barbarian the same cryptic answer as it gave the weaver:

"In time, all will be revealed."

~ ~ ~

# The Cavern

There was a routine to waking up: Waking in the stone room, Taunauk pulling a torch free, wandering the barren stretches of hall. Quiet companionship. The kindling of power in Helesys wand-arm.

Occasionally questions bubbled to the surface, but mostly, Helesys and Taunauk walked the stretch of hallway in silence. It was both purposeful, in the sense that they did not want to give away their position to potential enemies, and comfortable. Though they knew little about one another, Helesys realized that she still had a sense of the outlander, and, she imagined, Taunauk had a sense of her as well.

Taunauk was soft-spoken, wise beyond his Terran years, and practical in an animalistic sense. He was even more primal in combat, owed to his barbarian rage, and some other hidden, golden power that he was just beginning to understand.

Helesys suspected they got along so well, partly out of necessity, but partly because she sensed within herself the same practicality—that of a soldier, rather than an animal. But practicality, all the same. She suspected their practiced violence was also a bonding point.

In the gloom, Taunauk walked ahead of her, his wide shoulders blocking a great deal of the light and casting harsh shadows behind them.

Helesys followed, concealed beneath her cloak and the shadow of her comrade. Such was their marching order—Taunauk, the axe and shield. Helesys, the hidden dagger. She chuckled at the metaphor and thought that Shawn, their sporadic third comrade, would be jealous that he was not the dagger.

"What's so funny?" Taunauk asked quietly, without looking back.

"Just trying to explain how an outlander, a weaver, and a rogue wound up in a place like this."

Taunauk was silent a moment before answering. "Traveling together. Then we happened upon a trap or a curse that bound us to the dungeon."

"That seems logical, but then *why* were we traveling together?"

"Does it matter?"

"It could be a clue to who we were before the dungeon," Helesys said, "or it will be good to know once we escape and need to complete our business."

"*That* is a good point. I believe I was banished. Why would an elven weaver travel with a banished Endroggen?"

Helesys thought on this a moment, for they did make a strange pair. Even though Helesys didn't remember much about her life before, she knew that elves kept mostly to themselves. To hear Taunauk speak of the Endroggen, it seemed they did the same.

Finally, she said, "Perhaps you enlisted my help."

Taunauk grunted amusedly.

"What's so funny?" She asked, mocking his original question, and felt suddenly defensive. "Is it because I'm an elf or a female?"

"You are an elf," Taunauk said plainly, looking back over his shoulder in the flickering torch light. "Must have been some trouble to call upon the elves."

She smiled, relieved at the innocence of his remark. "The wizard, Amadeus, said that elven technology was advanced. Maybe your needs were arcane in nature? The minds of men were not enough."

"What of this... That you sought my help as a tracker. Your quarry fled into the wilderness and evaded your magic. Of course, Endroggen are the best trackers," the outlander said with a hint of jest.

"Quarry..." Helesys mused. "That is an interesting sentiment. It might explain what a group as unique as us would be together for."

"Then what about Shawn? How does the rogue figure into this?"

Taunauk grunted. "Then we are all banished."

"And a motley bunch we are," Helesys added. "Familiar too. I wonder if we had been traveling together long." She suspected that there was a purpose to the familiarity.

"A weaver, an outlander, and a rogue..." Taunauk grumbled idly.

Helesys added, "Chasing someone or being chased."

The two trailed off and walked in silence, for in the distance, the tunnel glowed softly. Some time later, the stone hallway opened up, giving way to an enormous cave.

Helesys thoughts drifted back to the flooded caverns of the fishmen and the enormous underground expanses lit by magical torches and littered with rust and ruins.

Here, the torches and fitted stones ended at the hallway, and gave way to jagged, moist rocks. Black rock lined the cavern and rose up hundreds of feet above them, dwarfing even those previous realms. The walls were covered in heaping swathes of glowing flowering plants—all manner of deep purples, blues and greens—which cast an eerie glow over the edges of the cavern. The air was humid to the point of haze—not quite to mist—and gave the far walls a surreal underwater glow. It was so high that the faint lights looked like smudged stars, but the hollow seemed to stretch out farther to the sides, as if the area was a massive tunnel.

Helesys and Taunauk stalked silently out from the hall, weapons ready and eyes darting across the glowing landscape, weary of any unseen dangers.

The only movement were ghostly creatures, barely more than a faint white outline and Helesys could scarcely make out more than the faintest of detail. Most walked on all fours, and faint outlines of horns and tails could be seen. Others looked Terran and walked on two legs. Of those, Helesys could make out arms and the smallest outline of a hand, but their face and fingers were barely a puff of mist. These ghostly creatures faded in and out of view as if they were made of mist itself, only appearing to stoop at a flower, disappear and reappear at another—as if the flowers somehow gave form to them.

When the creatures did not notice Helesys and Taunauk, the weaver turned her attention to the closest of the glowing flowers. The smallest were nearly two feet across, the largest were wider than she could reach across. Their shapes were alien and absurd—or so Helesys felt—and no two flower shapes or colors seemed to match. Each seemed utterly unique.

"What do you think of this, outlander?" Helesys asked.

Taunauk was studying the flowers similarly. He stowed the Everfall shield and reached into his bag for a small strip of bandage. He wrapped it around his fingers, then rubbed a broadleaf and petal of the nearest flower, then carefully smelled the cloth.

"It does not seem to be poisonous," he said reluctantly. "But give them a wide berth. We've seen too many strange sights to be sure that they are harmless."

Helesys nodded. That was good, at least. "Do they seem strange to you? *Otherworldly?*"

The barbarian nodded. "Yes. Very strange. Strange that we both are so certain, yet I can scarcely remember any flowers."

"So certain of our feelings…" Helesys trailed off and stared down the passageway. To the left, the cavern extended off into the distance, obscured by the heavy air and fading lights of distant plants. The right side of the cavern was darker, and in the gloom, she could just make out the regular pattern of a stone wall.

As Helesys set her sights on the distant stone wall, her gauntlet hummed with quiet reassurance.

She met Taunauk's eyes, and the barbarian nodded, an understanding passing between them. They would go to the right, and Taunauk would go first.

~ ~ ~

# The Gates

The pair stalked the edge of the cavern. There was a gentle slope to the walls, and Taunauk led them nearly as high on the edge as possible—mindful to stay hidden by the alien flowering plants as they went. For much of the walk, the mist-creatures seemed the only other creatures around. It wasn't until they stopped to rest and Helesys looked up again, that she saw the faintest glimpses of flying creatures in the gloom above.

Helesys pointed this out to her comrade. "What do you make of that?"

Taunauk eyed the creatures, glancing between the sky and the sprawling cavern floor. "They could be hunters."

"That would explain the lack of creatures below," Helesys added.

The outlander's eyes settled on the cavern floor and his eyes narrowed. "*Or* the hunters are down here." A moment later, he shrugged and added, "I would rather the hunters be down here—within axe-reach."

Helesys asked playfully, "What's the matter? Don't trust my gauntlet to keep flyers at bay?"

Taunauk smirked. "You've proven yourself many times over. No, I merely wish to earn my keep." He hoisted his axe for punctuation and led the way across the cavern.

As they walked, the stone wall came into view. It was a massive structure—one that stretched from wall to wall and floor to ceiling like a bulkhead. The blocks of the wall seemed made of the same shiny black texture as the rest of the cavern, save for their regularity. When they were within several hundred feet, the obscuring mist broke completely and they saw the lower swath of the wall in earnest. Ornate sculptures were chiseled into the lower two stories of the wall. Most of these were composed of a great coiling serpent, whose body roamed over the entire width of the wall. Terran faces and city outlines filled the spaces between the twisting coils.

At the center foot of the wall were a set of black stairs that rose up to an arch and large doorway.

Taunauk crouched and Helesys instinctively did the same, both hiding behind giant red petals. Then the barbarian pointed down the slope to the center of the cavern—to the first group of creatures they had seen.

There were six in total—two gray, mangy wolves and four Terrans: Two fishmen, absent weapons and shields, a ragged elven woman, and… Pitiful Lull. The last poor Terran walked in short strides, long limbs folded high like a bat. It was the first time that Helesys had seen Lull outside in such a manner; the sneaky Terran preferred confined spaces, darkness, and solitude.

"Something isn't right…" Helesys started to say.

Taunauk whispered, "Look at their faces."

Each of the Terrans and the wolves had the same thin, scabby 'X' that covered their faces. It was very faint and hard to see from so far away, but it was there. The heroes had seen the pattern before, back in the rusted prison of the fishmen's realm. There had been a prison cell full of diseased fishmen—infected by the parasite—whose faces had split in the same 'X'... The parasite was one of many *lingering deaths*.

The path forward lay through the stone doorway and there was little chance of sneaking around the group of infected to reach it.

"We can still turn back," Taunauk said.

"No," Helesys whispered. Though her wand-arm hummed with warning about the infected, she also felt that they needed to go through the doorway. She could not ignore the direction of the wand. It was leading them there for some reason, and she needed to know *why*.

"I will take out as many as I can," she said.

"Lull and the wolves will be quick," Taunauk replied, both as a recommendation and a warning.

Helesys took aim with her gauntlet, feeling the familiar build and churn of power. Purple lightning jumped across her fingers and coalesced around her palm. She fired, and a silent scream of arcane power raced across the cavern.

The blast collided with the group of infected, splitting one of the fishmen in red halves.

"*Stercus*," Helesys cursed. She had aimed for Lull, but at such a great distance, her accuracy was lacking.

She readied to fire again, and the faces of the infected split into a black, writhing mass. Their hisses rose to a screech, like a horrid song building to a crescendo. She fired again and the second beam crumpled the elven woman into a heap across the ground.

The rest of the infected sprinted toward them. The pair of wolves were quicker and led the charge, their paths crossing as the pair weaved toward Helesys and Taunauk. But Lull was just behind them, running on all fours, limbs stretching and folding in great, lurching strides.

Helesys fired again, aiming for the wolves up front. The blast soared across the rocks, tearing the tops off of three glowing plants, and smashed into one wolf, sending out a fine black mist of cursed blood.

Lull overcame the last wolf, crossing the rocks like a nightmare—covering a dozen feet with each stride. Helesys grit her teeth, dug deep and readied a spreadblast from her gauntlet—she wouldn't have time to aim.

Lull leapt the last thirty feet, soaring through the air with outstretched arms, its fingers splayed so wide they looked like a giant spider coming at her. And behind its hands, its face was split open wide in a black, writhing 'X'.

From beside her, a barbarian roared, and his battleaxe came down in a blur, striking the infected Terran twice in the span of his pass. Helesys dove out of the way, and Lull sailed past her. His arms and legs separated and tumbled past his body.

Helesys rose swiftly and turned her readied blast toward the second wolf, which was all but upon them. It leapt with a mix of hiss and snarl, and Helesys's spreadblast hit it like a wall of arcane power. It fell back, silent and mangled.

Meanwhile, the last fishman was only halfway to them, and, despite the carnage, running right toward them. Helesys fired one last shot, which sailed through the senseless creature.

Behind her, the infected Lull hissed for a moment longer, until Taunauk silenced it with his axe.

Silence fell over the cavern as Helesys and Taunauk collected themselves. The pungent stench of wet animal rose from the ground—from the spilled black blood.

"They don't have much sense about them," Taunauk said. He wiped the blade of his axe across one of the giant petals, and a trail of black blood remained on the flower. "They didn't even try to avoid your shots."

Helesys glanced at the severed remains of the infected Pitiful Lull, haphazardly laid arms and legs, and looked away. "They no longer have a will of their own. They only care about spreading the infection."

Taunauk grunted in agreement. "Creatures like that are dangerous. They cannot be bluffed or reasoned with."

"Then we will give them a wide berth," Helesys said, repeating the outlander's phrase.

Taunauk smirked and led them onward to the stone doors.

~

Helesys and Taunauk walked up the stairs to the stone doors and marveled at the sight. From up close, the stone wall that stretched across the cavern was truly staggering. Though it wasn't as big as the Infinite Wall, it was all the more impressive because it did not seem like it was made by the dungeon… Helesys felt that it was made by the inhabitants.

The doors themselves were nearly three stories tall and fashioned from single pieces of the obsidian block. From here, Helesys could also make out writing in between the sprawling design of the serpent and smaller designs seated in its coils. The script was comprised of squares and geometric patterns. The letters themselves were regular, but their sentences sprawled out in waves and spirals… Some even in designs resembling flower petals.

Taunauk approached the doors, cautiously eyeing the platform and the surrounding stone for traps or pressure plates. When he was satisfied, he stowed his axe and pushed against the two doors. He pushed for only a moment, the thick muscles of his calves coiling behind the straps of his grieves, but the doors did not move in the slightest.

"There must be another way," Helesys said idly, turning her attention to the carved words. *There must be.* Why else would her wand-arm lead them this way? Of all the warnings and direction, the wand had never steered them wrong before…

Helesys stepped closer and ran her metal fingers over the strange script. It was a gamble—her gauntlet seemed able to translate most languages, but the tongue spoken by the cannibals of the jungle had taken time to decipher…

But the words came to Helesys, whispered gently from the stone:

*We are but dreams. Dreams of the serpent Shéslang .*
*We walk and climb and fly, and dread to wake.*
*Dread to remember.*
*Only those that speak the soft tongue of Shéslang may enter.*
*Speak of dreams.*

Helesys walked as her fingers trailed over the sentence. She spoke the words aloud for Taunauk and then let her metal arm fall to her side. She knew without looking that the other scrawlings on the stone said the same thing. *Speak of dreams.*

"What dreams?" Helesys wondered aloud.

Taunauk glanced from the stone to the sprawling cavern behind them, keeping watch. "Can you speak the language?"

The weaver nodded. "I think so." And she called upon her wand to translate again. "*Ambula. Scandere. Volare...*" She spoke the words for *walk, climb*, and *fly*, but the stone did not respond. "*Serpentinen. Shéslang ...*" and the words for the serpent of legend. The stones sat idle.

Then she spoke, "*Somnia,*" the word for *dreams*, and the platform vibrated beneath their feet. The great stone doors slid with a grating sound, opening just wide enough for a Terran to walk through and no wider.

Barbarian and weaver stalked through the opening, and as soon as they passed over the threshold, the doors slid shut behind them.

~

Beyond the doors was a hallway full of silence and gloom. At first, the inside seemed completely dark, but when Helesys eyes adjusted, she could see the faintest blue glow from down the hall.

"Make your light," Taunauk whispered, pulling both Everfall and axe over head.

Helesys called upon her warding light, making it as dim as possible and keeping it at her comrade's back. She had nearly forgotten that Taunauk did not see quite as well in the dark as her.

For the briefest moment, Helesys was conflicted—whether to proceed quietly or whether to call out and announce themselves. Until she saw the dried coating of dark blood that covered the stones, the upper walls sprayed with droplets, while tacky puddles covered the floor. Stepping in the dried puddles released a musky odor.

"It is here too," Helesys said, kindling her wand-arm. She looked upon the hallway with different purpose and thought again of announcing their presence. "We can lure the parasites into the hall. My blasts will cut them down."

Taunauk grunted in affirmation. "I'm ready."

Helesys fired a single low-powered blast down the hall, the silent purple energy illuminating the bloody stones and several branching halls. The single-minded infected turned the corner and chased the impact of the blast. The singing came again—no more than a distant hum.

Helesys increased the power and felt her gauntlet grow warm with effort. She shot twice more. The purple shots tore across the hall and slammed into the backs of the creatures, bursting them like over ripened fruit—but not all of them.

Those that lived and the new ones that poured into the hall sang even louder. The shrill tone of the parasite echoed through the halls—so loud that Helesys didn't hear the scurrying feet as infected creatures trickled into the hall and half-sprinted, half-stumbled toward them. Terrans, wolves, spiders, giant lizards—all gaunt and desperate—their faces split wide and they began a writhing mass of black 'X's.

Helesys churned power and braced herself, heal and shoulder to stone. A hum of power built to a rattle, and the weaver launched repeater blasts down the hall. Dozens of creatures broke and burst in the wake of the blasts. Each blast sailed through and struck the stone at the end of the hall, shaking the structure like a giant drum. For a moment, Helesys was holding back the tide. But dozens more creatures filled their ranks, like a dam buckling and spilling over. The horde was pushing down the hall.

The weaver grit her teeth while the gauntlet rattled her shoulder. She pushed aside all thoughts of doubt and pain, and thought only of unleashing a torrent of her power. Meanwhile, Taunauk waited, half-crouched like a panther, and began to bounce on the balls of his feet in anticipation.

The first of the creatures descended upon them, a grotesque minotaur, face opened wide in parasitic infection. Taunauk lashed out with Everfall and smashed the beast against the hall with a horrid crunch. Taunauk recoiled and slashed with axe against a Terran that lunged, cleaving it from shoulder to ribs.

Helesys's shots sped up to a steady drumbeat, while Taunauk was timing his strikes, lashing out in between those short breaths of recoil. The pair became a single weapon—a single cliffside upon which the horde crashed against and time after time found itself repelled.

Until finally, the last two parasites fell beneath Taunauk's axe and shield.

Helesys leaned against the stone, her wand-arm so hot that she smelled the burning cloth of her cloak. Taunauk's chest heaved and the barbarian finally let his arms down to his sides. The pair stayed a moment while Helesys collected herself, neither needing to give voice to the reason, before continuing down the hall.

They stepped over the burnt and broken bodies, boots squelching in the sticky puddles.

As they walked, the soft blue lights at the end of the hall wavered, then grew brighter. Dozens of tiny faeries flew into the hallway, barely half-a-hand tall. Their bodies and wings glowing a brilliant blue. The pair watched cautiously and curiously as the faeries began cleaning the stone walls—wiping the black ichor from the faces of the carvings and leaving the rest untouched. The faeries were quick and diligent, working the stone clean in spiraling motions, from the outside to inside.

"Why do they do that?" Helesys wondered aloud. "The faeries in the fishmen temple did the same. Wiped the moss from the faces of the statues."

Taunauk had no reply. He merely watched with a mix of respect and caution, keeping one eye on the faeries and the other on the hall.

One faerie left the wall and flew to Helesys. The weaver held up her gauntlet in protest, but the faerie slipped around it and hovered in front of her face. In spite of the surprise, Helesys kept still, and the faerie cleaned the sprinkles of black blood from her face like a diligent mother. From so close, she saw plainly the barely contained electricity of their bodies, white lightning dancing inside a haze of blue. Helesys expected a shock from their touch, but was met with the sensation of thick velvet running over her face. Another faerie flew to Taunauk who watched with apprehension, wide eyes and hard lines of his face illuminated by blue light. But as the faerie cleaned the ichor from his face, he closed his eyes respectfully, as if he were receiving a sacrament.

Again, Helesys willed her gauntlet to translate—as it did with so many other languages—but she received only silence. The faeries were among the unknowable, like the fishmen and the parasites.

When Helesys and Taunauk's faces were clean, their faeries returned to the others, slowly cleaning their way down the hall. Helesys missed the warmth of its touch on her cheek. The tiny blue creatures left an eerie half-mess in their wake.

"What do they say?" Taunauk asked, finally opening his eyes.

"I do not know. I think there is a limit to the gaps it can bridge. Something so different cannot be explained in words."

Taunauk watched the faeries. "Or so simple it need not be translated. Hunger. Joy. Reverence… We all feel such things."

The weaver smiled. "I like that answer better."

~

Helesys and Taunauk followed the faeries, weapons ready yet with relative comfort, and mindful to step over the gore as they went. Being on the other end of her gauntlet meant a quick and usually gruesome fate for all but the strongest creatures.

If the parasite lingered here, then they had likely killed the last of them. Even though they had separate bodies, they acted with singular, simple purpose—to spread. Helesys gave quiet thanks to Movernus that the parasite did not know anything of tactics, for that would've made a terrible foe.

The hallway branched out into several other short lengths, each with small rooms off of them. There was little in them save for stone outcroppings in the shapes of beds and seating benches. The pair found the same gruesome scene continued in room after room, dried blood coating the already black stones—all with clean faces. The parasites had been trapped and left to fester like a tainted wound, while the faeries rested in small nooks around the ceiling. Helesys wondered whether the infected Terrans had left the small creatures alone. The faeries seemed completely content, regardless of who was passing by.

Helesys thought of the infected fishmen locked away in the rusted prison and how they were starved near to death. A horrid fate, even for the simple-minded.

The scrawling murals continued too, continuing on about the city and its rise from the walls of Shéslang's tunnel. Everything had come from the serpent's wake: Stone to build, plants to farm, weapons and gems from condensed magic. Much of the legends were repeated, and much in the sense of poetry. Helesys sighed—none of it was useful to the heroes.

Save for a single room. More writing adorned the walls; Written in short, shallow strokes. It was mangled and haphazard… or the writing of someone in a panic.

*All is lost. Don't go into the city. Don't go. Don't go.*

Then to the corner of the room: *Check under the floor plate. Take only one statue. Only one.* The elf read the words aloud for Taunauk.

The barbarian glanced back down the hall, the way they came. "They got through," he said solemnly. "Gods, what awaits us."

Helesys said nothing and stooped down to the floor where the last bit of writing led. Soft remnants of magic emanated from the floor. She felt around the stones of the corner and one wobbled. She pried up on it and it came away easily, revealing a tiny cubbyhole in the floor. Inside were half a dozen brown sacks—empty—save for one.

Helesys opened the bag and found several small, carved totems, each resembling a different animal: An elephant made of marble, an obsidian dog, a pair of silver lions, three ivory goats, and a jade lemur. Helesys thumbed the totems with her gauntlet.

*Only one…*

Though each resonated with magic, only one totem brought an image to her mind's eye. Through some unspoken message from her wand, she knew that only one of them could fly.

"Something neither of us can do," Helesys said—she picked the jade lemur, and placed the other totems and sacks back into the hole, and the stone on top of it. She pocketed the lemur and felt a soft spark of magic from it.

"We could turn back," Taunauk whispered. "The parasite is a lingering death."

Helesys stood and turned to face her comrade. The butt of his axe rested on the ground and Taunauk leaned wearily on it—for the first time, Helesys saw worry upon his face.

Scrawled ominously on the door above him was more jagged writing. *Duoausongur*, repeated three times. *Death song…* The civilization's name for the parasite. She told this to Taunauk.

"I feel this is the way to go," she said plainly. "The wand guides me." It was such a subtle feeling that she wondered if it hadn't been guiding her through all the realms.

The barbarian said nothing. He merely stared down the short hallway, looking toward the branching paths.

Helesys remembered when he'd been mangled by the many hands of Shomosk—another lingering death in Zhug's crypt. He'd leapt ferociously at the beast… but that was before they knew of the lingering deaths and just how close Taunauk had come to being lost forever.

"I do not ask this lightly," she started to say.

"I trust you," Taunauk replied. He stood straight and held his axe in one hand. "If one of us should get infected… Do not hesitate. I will not become one of those things. I will do the same for you."

She wanted to say that she already knew what to do—that she had already done so once before during their time in the Wode. Back when Taunauk had been run through by the Green Knight's blade and nearly turned into one of the birch-men.

So it was twice… Twice that her friend had nearly succumbed to a lingering death. Now she was asking him to brave such a fate again—he who knew it best.

The only words she could find were, "And I trust you."

~ ~ ~

# The Hellish Skyline

Helesys and Taunauk walked the hall to the end, to where Helesys's blasts had sailed through the first infected and sailed into the far wall. Despite the blasts, the far wall was unscathed, and contained the entrance to the city proper. The seam was thin, but easy enough to see where it bisected the ornate carvings.

There were no more depictions of the serpent. There was only the skyline of the City of Shéslang. Ornate peaks and towers rose and fell majestically, and though they were etched in the black stone wall, they called forth images of the spines, petals, stalks, and bright colors of the plants outside—a jewel in the gloom.

But whatever beauty the carvings and her imagination belied, there were soft whispers from beyond the stone—the faintest voices of the parasite. Of vile song boiling through the seam in the door.

*Speak of dreams*, the writing on the door said. *Speak the word and live in the bosom of Shéslang.*

"*Somnia*," Helesys said, speaking the old word for *dream*, heart pounding in her throat. Her wand-arm thrummed in demand and in dire warning. Only the kindling of power seemed to calm it, though it did little to still the weaver.

Taunauk took a step in front of her, Everfall and axe in hand, ready for whatever horrors lay beyond.

The stones rumbled and clacked against their confines before sliding open. The gloom of the hall and the beautiful, etched skyline of the stones parted.

The smell of seeping rot hit them like a wave, and the singing grew to a scream. Piercing. Shrill.

The flowering skyline of the city was replaced with a twisted, writhing mass, the imagined colors of flowers replaced with slick black and oozing shades of purple. The parasite had spread and covered the city. Only in isolated places did some peaks of white stone rise through the mass—the remnants of buildings—sitting like icebergs on a black sea.

The dream of Shéslang was replaced with the nightmare of the parasite.

The short platform and descending stairs in front of Helesys and Taunauk were mercifully untouched, but even in those few moments, the writhing tentacles turned toward them. It was as if the eyes of thousands of infected turned upon them.

"Great Movernus…" Taunauk whispered.

Helesys reached for the jade lemur and grasped it with her metal hand, searching for the magic words.

"*Messoris umbra, matris' vellus, ventus equitem!*"

The totem pulsed and slipped from Helesys's grasp. It fell to the ground, the green rock elongating and forming limbs. The jade lemur was quickly waist high and seconds later its shoulders were as tall as Helesys. Fur sprouted from the stone, its short snout twisted toward them in a curious glare.. The deep brown color was the last to change, turning into a shade of earth and near-white stripes that ran down its back. Thick webs of skin stretched from its forelimbs to its thighs. Its eyes stared the same bright green color of jade.

Knowing that the beast would heed her commands, Helesys grasped its furry flank and pulled herself up to sit on top of its shoulders. The beast howled, high and guttural, but merely crouched in anticipation, and Helesys felt the physical and magical power coiling within the beast.

The weaver turned to the outlander. "Up is the only way."

Taunauk grunted in reservation, but hoisted himself up onto the back of the lemur.

Meanwhile, the writhing ichor of the parasitic city was climbing the stairs. Masses of sludge and flesh lurched toward them—a blending of tentacle and maw, snapping and gurgling.

"*Volare, pueri,*" Helesys commanded in the old words. *Fly, child.*

The lemur unfurled its forelimbs and wings, and stretched them to their full length, clear across the platform. Thin spines of cartilage stretched back from its arms, giving depth to its wings. In one sheer motion, the lemur leapt and beat its powerful arms, and soared into the air. Helesys seized the thick fur on its back and leaned forward as it carried the heroes up into the air.

For a moment, the suddenness of flight scared her, but Helesys soon felt a connection between her and the beast. Magic held her to its back, just as magic compelled the lemur to heed her commands. How powerful this connection was, she could not say—only that Helesys was not willing to let go with both hands and completely trust in the power of the spell.

Above them, they found the familiar glow of alien flowers and gloom of darkness between. Once they were safe and high enough, the lemur leveled off its flight. Only then could Helesys look back to check on her comrade, and found a faint smile on his face at the marvel of flight.

The city writhed and screamed below them. Some of the topmost towers even reached their altitude. From below, these white towers had seemed like untouched reaches. But as the heroes flew by, they found thin veins of ichor reaching up the peaks, and the frail tendrils reached out to them as they passed.

The cavern stretched on, as did the black city. So they flew, neither speaking, for even that high up the screams of the *Duoausongur* were deafening.

~

The pair flew in silence on the lemur while the cursed city stretched on. The cavern began to curve and twist, and the city followed it. Somewhere, there might have been breaks in the skyline or streets weaving back and forth, but now there was only the *Duoausongur*—the parasite had engulfed everything.

Everything except for the black rock of the cavern. Some hundred feet up the walls, evidence of the parasite disappeared, and the glow of the alien flowers took over. Perhaps it could not climb the rock or perhaps some lingering magic kept the parasite at bay. Regardless, Helesys was grateful for the small respite.

They had flown for an hour, and through half a dozen turns of the cavern, when they noticed movement in the gloom above them. Winged shadows appeared and disappeared just as quickly.

Helesys steered the lemur to the left, to an alcove on the cavern wall. The weaver and barbarian leapt to the stone, weapons already drawn and readied, while their mount shrunk to the stone, hiding itself from whatever circled above.

They waited, but none of the shadows descended.

Helesys grit her teeth and grew impatient. "What do you make of this?"

Taunauk stared at the gloom, his eyes only half-following the shadows. "Could be predators… But most have the sense not to be seen before they strike."

Meanwhile, the lemur stayed focused on its newfound masters. It seemed content to stay crouched beneath the alcove and offered no sound or movement in protest.

They waited until Helesys could bear it no longer. "There is only one way to be sure," she said, turning back to their lemur. "Let us make our presence known."

Taunauk nodded, and they both leapt on their lemur.

Helesys willed the creature upward and it heeded her, climbing at a furious pace. From so high up, the screams of the parasite were drowned out by the mist and the vastness between them.

For a moment, it looked as if the shadows scattered, but the shadows returned, zipping from the walls of the cavern to and fro. They slipped into view, dozens of other flying lemurs. They wore the same dark fur, but their backs and stomachs were covered with mottled patches of white, and some were even bigger than the heroes' mount.

The creatures circled round, whooping and hollering. Larger lemurs circled past, diving and reaching out with their dextrous back feet. Helesys commanded their lemur to evade, and it twisted, dove, and rose to stay out of reach. The other lemurs seemed just as distraught at the sight of the mount and focused on it just as much as they did at Helesys and Taunauk.

Meanwhile, the weaver's gauntlet grew warm with power and with understanding, giving voice to their growls and chattering.

*"False-lemur."*

*"Infidel."*

*"Half-hair."*

*"Made-thing."*

There were too many. Six lemurs accosted them in the air, while more clung to the walls and shouted encouragement and violence.

Rather than unleash the violence of her gauntlet, Helesys bolstered her strength and her voice. Her wand translated her words into the guttural language of the lemurs. She boomed, *"This made-thing is mine! Death to the first who touches us and to as many more as we can take with us."*

At this, the lemurs grew discordant. *"The hairless devil speaks our tongue!"*

Another cursed them as, *"That-which-should-not-fly."*

The lemurs backed away as they cursed, and for the moment it looked as if Helesys's threat had spared them.

Finally, the group scattered and the largest of the shadows floated down. The lemur was gargantuan—nearly twice the breadth of their mount. Nearly all the brown had gone from its body, leaving a ghastly mass of white fur. Its wingbeats were slow and powerful, and massive swathes of air were displaced with each beat.

Helesys felt the weariness of her lemur, the primal fear, and had to quell its urge to flee. Still, the larger beast matched their speed and altitude with ease.

And when it spoke, she felt its voice shake her chest. *"Wanderers, the made-thing is not welcome in our sky."* Enlarged fangs glittered in the twilight, in a mouth wide enough to swallow a Terran whole.

Helesys stared at the beast and left the threat from her voice. *"We seek passage through the cavern. Then we shall remove the made-thing from your sky."*

The great beast paused and stared across the cavern as it flew, then turned its attention back to them. *"The cavern's end is treacherous. It is forbidden to fly there."*

*"We are not lemurs,"* Helesys replied. She was kindling power, her mind weighing just how powerful a blast would be needed to knock the beast from the sky should it turn on them.

The giant lemur coughed, a deep and harsh rumble that shook the sky like thunder. *"It is forbidden because it is dangerous. It is madness. You might as well fall here and die in the maw of the parasite."*

*"We will go,"* Helesys said firmly.

Four more lemurs descended, each as big as the last—each taking a position to their flank.

Taunauk growled behind her and Helesys felt the mount's fear grow, once again taking her concentration to calm it.

One of the new lemurs rumbled, *"The Missives desire the wanderers' presence."*

The largest lemur laughed again, the booming sounds causing even the other giant lemurs to startle. *"Tell her yourself."*

~ ~ ~

# Summoned by the Missives

Helesys and Taunauk followed the giant lemurs deeper into the cavern. They rose even higher into the air, leaving the city of the *Duoausongur* far below and relegated to a whisper.

Now they were completely surrounded by the indigenous lemurs, which followed not just in the sky but also scurried along the walls. Hundreds of eyes turned toward Helesys, Taunauk and their own flying lemur. The pungent smell of wet fur hung in the air.

They passed small tunnels cut into the rock that lined the cavern. Smaller lemurs threaded through the tunnels and stopped to see the spectacle of the *hairless devils* and their *made-thing*.

Helesys no longer bothered to kindle her wand-arm, for she had to focus nearly all her concentration on keeping their mount from panicking. At first, Helesys wondered if the lemurs presented so grave a danger, but her gauntlet's warnings were minimal. So she suspected the jade lemur's discomfort must have something to do about a made-thing being around so many of its real counterparts.

She tried to think back to their time in the Deacon's village in the Wode, about Perdita and how the young woman had been a made-thing. The Deacon had used magic to make a child from the flesh of another. Had Perdita been as nervous or felt as different as their jade lemur felt now? The young channeler had certainly spent more time outside of the village than inside it.

Perdita had known *what* she was—knew that she was a made-thing. But the people of the village hadn't treated her differently. In fact, the villagers had looked upon Perdita and the Deacon with a mix of awe and reverence… and a smattering of fear. The fear was small and quiet, but unmistakably there.

It mattered little, since there was little chance that they would ever be reborn in the Wode, little chance that she could ever ask Perdita about it. Even less chance that the young channeler would answer her.

So up they rose, to the utmost heights of the cavern—heights that should've been dizzying, save for the obscuring mist that reduced the parasite-covered city to a haze of black and red.

The largest lemur, the one who laughed, clung to the wall, shoving smaller lemurs out of its way. It looked to a small tunnel nearby. "*Land there and follow the warren. They will lead you to the Missives. Go in peace and you shall leave in peace.*"

Helesys bid their lemur to land and when they dismounted, she considered recalling the creature to its jade statue form, but some other feeling inside prevailed. Two smaller lemurs, their fur nearly black and spotless, led the way through the tunnels.

Taunauk and Helesys followed, with the jade lemur just over her shoulder.

The tunnel was barely wider than Helesys's outstretched arms, noticeably tight for the jade lemur, and the stone changed from smooth lines to scaled patterns. The air grew dry and warm.

The stone beneath their feet gave way to tightly packed, dark red dirt. At the end, the tunnel opened to a chamber just some ten feet square. Slithering shapes were cut into the stone—waves or tree branches—and three lemurs laid about the curves on the wall. Their bodies were long and slender and seemed almost like snakes perching on the stones. Their ears were pulled back, laying nearly flat against the scalp. They were the same color as the stone and gave the illusion that they were rising from it.

"*Stand before us,*" the middle one said in a raspy voice.

Helesys and Taunauk stood in the center of the room and Helesys willed the jade lemur to stand with them. Interestingly, this task became easier than when they had been surrounded outside by the giants and the crowd. The only lemurs inside with them were the three elders and the black, spotless lemurs, who paced around the back of the room; their menace was a quieter form, though no less deadly to the trained weaver.

The three old lemurs stared with deep purple eyes, regarding each of the two heroes and made-thing lemur with equal attention.

"*Wanderers…*"

"*Indifferent…*"

"*Made-thing…*"

As they whispered, Helesys found their mouths moved little, and it became hard to keep track of which one spoke.

*"We seek passage,"* Helesys interjected. She felt the tense eyes of the black lemurs behind her—as if she spoke out of turn.

*"We have survived this long because we have kept the likes of you away,"* the right-most replied.

*"Yet you brought us here,"* she replied.

Whispers or grumbles passed between them. *"They seek Shéslang."*

*"Yes…"*

*"Yes… But you will not make it through the Column, to the upper-most reaches of the cavern."*

*"What power does it hold?"* Helesys interjected again. *"I am drawn to it."*

Whispers passed between the elders again. *"Drawn to a god…"*

*"Aren't we all…"*

*"We have not seen it… Never seen it."*

*"Hallowed ground. Go and never return here."*

*"Wait,"* the left-most lemur said, and the others fell silent. *"I called them here. Let me see the made-thing."*

Helesys commanded the jade lemur to step forward, and had it placed before the three elder lemurs. They chattered silently, save for the left one, who coughed sporadically. Helesys wand-arm registered it as sadness.

The left lemur's breathing grew hoarse and with great effort it rolled its body on the winding platform. The elder's back was light brown with several white stripes running down the length—the same as the jade lemur. It rolled back on the rocks to face the group.

*"My likeness,"* the elder said. *"Long ago, the city and our kind lived together. But when the parasite came, we retreated and left the Terrans to their fate. In the final days, they used the last of Shéslang's magic to cast weapons and trinkets… But nothing would save them. Not even*

*the serpent itself. If you find Shéslang, I want you to ask it why,"* the elder said. *"Why didn't it save the city and its people?"*

The center lemur raised a spindly arm, calling silence to the room. *"You would not like the answer, Missive. Go. Go now and do not return. Our children will let you pass. Others in the cavern will not show such kindness."*

The left lemur said quietly, *"Do not squander the gift."*

The heroes nodded but offered no further reply. They turned and followed the dark lemurs out the way they came. Helesys whispered to Taunauk, summarizing the strange conversation. Outside, lemurs clung to the cavern walls in respectful silence. None chattered or shouted insults at the jade lemur—as if the Missives had bestowed some blessing upon them or simply that their leaving was blessing enough.

Helesys and Taunauk leapt atop their mount and the jade lemur flew from the outcropping, leaving a hundred quiet, curious stares behind.

~

They flew some hour more in silence before stopping to rest and to eat on a small outcropping. The jade lemur shrunk down to the corner while Helesys and Taunauk sat closer to the edge. The lemur's tail curled around Taunauk's waist, which the barbarian paid no mind to.

They ate strips of jerky while the quiet, discordant song of the parasite struggled to rise above the mist. Twice, Helesys offered a sliver of jerky to the jade lemur, but it didn't so much as smell the offering.

Helesys turned her attention to her wand-arm, holding it at length and looking the shiny mithral up and down. "So much forgotten and so little returned to us."

"Do you remember anything else? Anything about your arm?" Taunauk asked.

The weaver shook her head. "Guesses. I think I was injured and my arm was replaced with this one. That it happened on the battlefield. I remember blastshells raining down… and I am terrified of them. The kind of deep fear that comes with reason. You?"

Taunauk reached a hand back to his axe and pulled it overhead. He set it across his thighs and grasped the handle tightly. "It is familiar. It echoes, as it did that first time we woke in the dungeon. It is old and the grip is worn. Likely an heirloom. Likely from my father or another elder of the tribe…"

"What is it?"

Hesitantly, he replied, "All the more strange that I was outcast and allowed to keep it. *Aonar* is the name of the clanless. The name of an outcast."

The weaver smiled, a kindling of reassurance. "In the Wode, I lamented the ease with which violence came to me. I feel I was a soldier and that those ways do not serve me now. It was strange to have no memory of my old life and yet want to distance myself from it. What defined me then does not define me now—*you* said that. Whatever your transgressions, whatever your penance, you are not the same man."

"Kind words… But you worried that our memories will remake us. What of that?"

"I do not feel that we will become the Terrans that we were, no matter how much comes back to us. We have traveled far without our memories and become new along the way. We have made ourselves… Perhaps becoming trapped here was a gift," she added coyly.

Taunauk met her eyes, found jest, and the pair laughed.

When the barbarian had finished laughing, he said, "Those were Shawn's words from your lips."

"You go too far!" Helesys chuckled. When their laughter smoldered, she added, "He should be here. It is not right for one to be alone like that."

"Agreed. One day, when our power has become great, we will make it so he is reborn with us."

"One day… We will not perish at all."

~

Helesys and Taunauk flew on the back of the jade lemur for hours, through twists and turns that seemed never ending. The glowing flowers, the dark, obscuring mist, and the distant song of the parasite-infested city below were their only companions. The unchanging landscape drew on and became maddening.

"Look," Taunauk said.

Helesys glanced back and saw her comrade pointing upward. Above them, glowing flowers and black rock came into view. At first, this seemed strange, since Helesys had willed the beast to keep constant flight within the tunnel.

But it wasn't just the ceiling—the sides of the cavern seemed closer as well. The tunnel was still some thousand feet wide, but the sides no longer disappeared completely into the mist. Now the glow of climbing plants surrounded them. And below the screams of the *Duoausongur* grew.

The tunnel was shrinking and seemed to be doing so right before their eyes as they flew deeper into it.

"We have to keep going," Helesys called over the wind and the growing screams from below.

Taunauk said nothing, but she heard the slip of the axe from his backsling.

In the clouds, something terrible grew. Instead of the blue, green glow that had become a comforting sign of altitude and safety, a shadow grew in the mist. Like a dark moon rising.

At first, the circle was only a dozen feet across, but it quickly dwarfed the wingspan of their mount. Meanwhile, the tunnel shrank until it looked like the two would converge and their path would be completely blocked.

Only when the shadow began to glow an iridescent red, did Helesys feel the surprise and dread of the jade lemur. She willed the beast to continue, and then the mist broke completely.

The cavern was engulfed in an oozing, pulsing red and black mass. Thick fibers of cartilage and sinew pulled and writhed, splaying maws of jagged black teeth open and shut in discordant breath. In scant places, bright white peaks shone through—the parasite, in all its horror and glory, had climbed this high monument of the City of Shéslang, and completely engulfed it. Great flailing arms stretched out to the stone limits of the tunnel. At the ends of which were mixtures of hands and mouths, their twisted shapes plucking flesh from the glowing plants, even tearing some free and throwing them to the parasite city below.

With the mass came the putrid smell of death and decay, and the song, and all of it washed over Helesys and Taunauk and the jade lemur. This song was different. No longer did Helesys hear the incomprehensible, discordant melody. Now the screams of the *Duoausongur* coalesced, slamming rhythmically into them in tidal wave bellows.

Deep fear grew in Helesys's gut and her jaw dropped open—for she understood the words!

*I HUNGER.*
*I HUNGER.*
*I HUNGER.*

Each short sentence fell with a crash, and she felt the maws and tendrils and things that might have been eyes turned toward the heroes—she felt the entire city turn and lurch below them.

The bold part of the weaver fell silent, for there was no fighting this horror. Even the most powerful blast from her wand-arm, at best, would recoil and knock them and their lemur from the sky

"Helesys flee!" Taunauk shouted, breaking Helesys from her trance.

The jade lemur banked in the air, its powerful wings pulsing just out of reach of the giant's tendrils. Behind her, a barbarian grunted and slashed his axe through one of the pursuing arms, and she felt the mount lurch beneath her. They could not fight in the air, not on the back of the lemur, and not over so perilous of a fate!

Helesys churned power and scanned the titan. There were openings between the mass and the edges of the cavern, but most were far too thin and others were lined with a landscape of gnashing teeth. Blasting through such masses would be too risky.

The jade lemur turned through the air again, swooping back the way it came. Two pointed arms descended on them and both were repelled with a slash of an axe and a blast of Helesys's arm. They could not stay in so perilous a spot, yet

Helesys felt the unmistakable urging of the magic wand. Something lay on the other side—at the end of the cavern—and she would not be denied.

An outcropping of rock and tunnel descending into darkness. They dove for it. The writhing titan's song shifted a fraction of a pitch in recognition of fleeing prey.

Helesys, Taunauk, and lemur hit the rock hard and rolled down the tunnel. Helesys commanded the lemur to shrink and in the rolling, she felt the small jade stone return to her hand, then pocketed the statue. Weaver and barbarian braced themselves, and turned back with weapons drawn.

But the parasite didn't come for them. None of the maws or claws dripping ichor… Nothing followed.

~ ~ ~

# *Mirror of Orrorim*

Taunauk led them through twisting catacombs with the light of Helesys's gauntlet at his back. Helesys kept the light burning low and kindled the rest of her power for whatever lurked in the flickering shadows.

She had felt it immediately—a sense of being watched, of being followed. As if something was lurking behind every crack and corner. The elf's hair stood on end, fighting a constant shiver from the unseen visage. She had felt the touch of scrying before—the wizard Amadeus's touch had been so subtle as to be invisible, while the giant Zhug's gaze had been so strong as to be oppressive.

But this touch was something else… Like uninvited breath upon the neck and coarse whisper in the ear. Chill upon her skin. Violating. Perverse. No amount of kindled power pushed away the feeling or the touch of the creeping mind that lurked in the darkness with them.

"Something is here," she whispered, trying to keep her voice from shaking.

"I feel it," Taunauk said quietly. "It is faint... But malevolent."

"It does not feel faint to me."

This caused the barbarian to pause. "There is a branch up ahead. We shall take whichever leads closer to Shéslang's cavern. We will not linger," he said sternly.

They passed the first branch, and it brought her back to the catacombs of the buried hive. The feeling grew louder—the weaver's gaze flit from tunnel to tunnel as they passed intersections. Each way she looked were shadows and darkness. Her distress grew—she could feel it growing closer. Something she could not see. A feeling she could not stop.

"We should turn back," she whispered, throat tight.

"Bolster your strength."

Helesys breathed deep and tried to split her concentration three ways. She could not lose the light, nor was she willing to give up a powered blast. Strength flowed to her muscles, to her chest, and she felt her resolve grow—if only slightly. The cold, the creeping touch, receded. It felt as if she had slipped a thin shell or cloth over her armor.

But *it* was still there. The feeling picked at her defenses, like a fingernail at a scab.

They passed two more intersections beset by shadows and darkness, with nothing but the sound of soft steps and measured breath.

To the right, they saw the soft green glow of salvation at the end of the tunnel. And she heard footsteps to her left.

Heart pounding, Helesys whirled around and brought her gauntlet and light to bear.

Taunauk stood a few paces away down the tunnel, hand over his eyes, axe hoisted in his other hand. "Helesys, get away from it!"

Again, the weaver spun and found Taunauk standing to her right as well, both Everfall and axe in hand. The glow of the Shéslang's cavern in the distance.

She looked at both and found them identical.

The barbarian to her right, the one she'd been following, growled and said, "Do not trust that *thing*."

Helesys grit her teeth, for she could not trust her senses. One of them was not what it seemed. One of them was that which crept over her. And so the weaver took a step away from the light, and held her gauntlet close, should she need to turn it against either outlander.

"We were heading back to the serpent's cave," Helesys said. "Why should I trust you that comes from darkness?"

"The light is an illusion," the Taunauk in darkness said.

From her right, the first Taunauk replied, "We were going toward the light. To the cavern of the Shéslang."

"We were born in darkness," the newcomer to the left said. "Remember the blastshells... The light is an illusion."

Taunauk to the right, stared at her, his face softening. When she did not move, he added, "You are Helesys of Great House Byyra—"

"You remember dancing in the great hall," Taunauk in the darkness said. He no longer shielded his eyes, and instead held out his hand, offering it. "You remember your mother and sister, Wynbella and Aradi. *Your hair*, Helesys. Your hair—"

"Enough!" Helesys glanced at both outlanders, anger twisting her face. The weaver flared her power and focused on the wand's innate sense of magic—hoping that it would help discern the truth.

For a moment, she *saw* them—a psychic depiction of them. Gnarled blue hands picking at her defenses, blue lips that had breathed on her neck and whispered in her ear.

Now that Helesys knew, she turned her magic to countering that of the creature. With fuming whisper, she cast them out of her mind and away from her thoughts, *"Get away from me!"*

And to her left, Taunauk that stood in darkness changed. Ripples of blue flashed across his skin and clothes.

The real Taunauk stepped defiantly to her side, eyes boring into the creature.

The axe disappeared from Fake-Taunauk's hand, but otherwise the creature kept up the illusion, despite its rippling facade. "She is powerful," the creature said in a whisper that echoed through the caverns.

*"Yes, she is,"* whispered a dozen other voices from behind.

And from the shadows came a dozen more Terrans. Their skin was deep blue, thin and saggy at the joints. Their faces were absent noses, mouths and ears, their bodies sexless. The creatures crouched and stood, clambering over one another behind Fake-Taunauk to glimpse at them, milky white eyes shining like dozens of ghostly jewels.

Another appeared, and this time Helesys's jaw hung slack—for she was staring at herself. Fake Helesys stepped to the front of the group, wearing her cloak and mithral chain mail, light glittering off her metal fingers. Her own Elven eyes stared back at her.

The illusion only stoked anger in the weaver. "Why continue the charade? We know what you are."

"Why do you wander? Why do you fight?" Fake-Helesys asked, face scrunched in arrogance.

"Because we must."

"Why do you assume it is any different for us?" Fake-Helesys replied. Beside her, Fake-Taunauk turned completely blue and turned back into its true form. "We are what we are… Can you imagine what it was like to be alone? Years without

the comfort of another. Without memories to survive on…
We lived in secret among the City of Shéslang and they knew
no better."

"I know what you do," Helesys corrected.

Fake-Helesys continued unperturbed, "We never used to
take so brazenly. One memory here, another there. Many parts
to make a whole." The creature looked upon itself and mumbled, "Not like this." She turned back to Helesys. "We are so
desperate. There are so many of us now… and so few to *take*
from."

At once, the weaver felt the creatures pushing back against
her countering magic. The thin psychic armor she'd donned
was ripped from her as the minds of a hundred creatures descended upon her. Cold swept over her skin, their prying touch
slipped under her scalp.

Helesys screamed and turned her gauntlet down the tunnel
and unleashed a blast that ripped chunks of stone from the
cavern and smashed into the gathered creatures. Blue blood
splashed across the walls.

The light of her gauntlet faded to a candle's warmth—she
had dumped so much power into her blast so quickly.

In the gloom and the gore, she saw dozens more white eyes
and blank faces staring back at her.

Taunauk seized her arm, and she saw fear writ large across
the barbarian's face. "Run!"

The pair sprinted through the tunnel, toward the light of
the serpent's cavern. Helesys bolstered the strength of her legs,
and she kept on the barbarian's heels.

But the chill touch of the creatures pawed at her back, at
her neck, and behind them hundreds of wet steps echoed
through the tunnel. Gaining on them.

Helesys pulled the jade lemur statue from her pocket. "*Reaper's shadow, mother's down, wind rider!*"

The lemur sprouted from the statue and when they were at the end of the tunnel, the edge of the cliff, they leapt onto its back and into the air.

~ ~ ~

# The Ends of
# the Serpent

Helesys and Taunauk flew on the back of the jade lemur, back into the maelstrom of lingering death. Their ill-fated detour through the caverns of the blue creatures had deposited them on the other side of the colossal parasite that covered the tallest monument in the city. Though they had passed through the most perilous section of Shéslang's cavern, their hardships were far from over.

There were more towers in this portion of the city. With each, the parasite rose to the same dangerous heights. As the heroes flew over the demented cityscape, the great flailing arms of the parasite lashed out at them.

Atop their mount, Helesys could not conjure the full might of her blasts, so she charged her wand-arm and fired smaller, repeating blasts at the tendrils. The writhing flesh tore and broke, and, always, more filled their ranks. She called on the ring of winter to bolster her shots and she rained down a gale of frost and destruction upon the tormented city.

Helesys thought of nothing except the barrage of power, as if she were riding a lightning storm and it was all she could do to aim it.

When the parasite grew close, reaching toward them with hands and maws and mixes of both, Taunauk lashed out with his battleaxe and cut them down. The jade lemur, a construct of will and magic, sprinted through the cascade of twisted flesh, banking and diving—never faltering, never tiring.

And the song of *hunger* grew ever louder.

Onward they flew, tempting lingering death. An unstoppable force slipping the grasps of an insatiable landscape.

~

The mighty towers did not last—they had passed the epicenter of the parasite and the city shrank beneath them again. The grasp of the parasite sank into the mist, like a Terran beneath the waves. In the final minutes of struggle, Helesys had kindled her strength and endurance to make it through.

But there was no rest, for the end of the tunnel approached.

*Where do we go from here?* But Helesys's thought was answered before she gave breath to it, for the cavern rose upward.

It was as if a hole opened up in the sky, narrower than before; instead of the walls being so wide that they were shrouded in mist, Helesys could see the bounds of the cavern above them.

*Up,* she bid the jade lemur, and they rose into the mist, unsure of what lay beyond.

Slowly, the mist parted, and revealed a column filled with glowing plants, so tall that it shrunk to a pinprick in the distance—so tall that it should've stretched to the surface of the realm.

Up and up they rose, holding on tight to the jade lemur as its mighty wings dragged them upward through the cavern.

Smaller tunnels permeated the walls, tunnels barely wide enough for a man. Helesys thought of the tunnels of the blue creatures and shuddered at the still-fresh memory.

Her fears were answered from below by the bellowing song of the *Duoausongur*. And then from all around.

As the trio rose in the air, a procession of creatures marched from the tunnels—elves, human, fishmen, slithering, lurching. They lined the edges of the vertical cavern and joined in the song. As far as Helesys could see above them, the walls seemed to squirm with movement, as if the entire length of it was alive. Then the faces of all of them split, revealing a writhing face of infection beneath, and the song of hunger rose through the cavern.

And they leapt from the walls.

The lemur slipped through the air, propelling itself upward and twisting through the oncoming bodies, but more and more leapt, following their cursed brethren. The rain of the parasite fell and became torrential, blotting out the glowing walls above them.

Helesys churned power and blasted upward, carving them a path. Taunauk slashed those that came near enough to touch, slicing them in half two and three at a time.

Up and up they rose, slaughtering their way through the current—Until the world was a deluge of bodies and Helesys bid the lemur to dive into the tunnels once again.

The lemur turned toward the nearest tunnel, which swarmed with faces of the parasite. Helesys churned power and blasted through a dozen of them. They landed in the rocky passage; the lemur slinking against the wall between its masters, while Taunauk and Helesys held off the swarm in the tunnel. The barbarian met them with Everfall and axe, while the weaver slipped her gauntlet around him and fired down the passage—the pair were a bastion against the screaming dark.

When the thickest rain was over, they leapt back onto the jade lemur and back into the cavern. With the deluge over, the lemur sprinted upward, and the trio slipped the last of the falling bodies with ease.

Before long, they climbed the narrowing tunnel with ease.

~

When the rain of infected finally ceased and the song of the *Duoausongur* fell to silence, the cavern still remained. Helesys estimated it must have stretched upward another mile. All the while, the walls of the cavern closed in around them.

Finally, the rocky end of the cavern came into view. At the very precipice, the cavern was roughly twenty feet across—barely wide enough for the jade lemur to fly. The direction turned sharply to a horizontal passage and continued off into the distance.

Helesys directed the jade lemur to land in the passageway. The outlander and the elf stared into the black, waiting with weapons poised.

But nothing came for them.

After the long moment passed and the pair finally relaxed, Helesys bid the lemur to turn back into its trinket form. The unfaltering, unflinching made-thing stared deep into her eyes.

Without protest, it shrunk to the ground, becoming hairless and small, until it was once again the jade statue that Helesys had claimed.

The weaver stooped to the ground, picked it up and cradled it. "*Omnis gratias*," she whispered.

"Good choice taking a flying mount," Taunauk said. The barbarian's cloak was covered in the black blood of the parasite. He slipped it off, wiped his face, and cast the cloak over the side.

Helesys watched him do it, then chuckled as she realized she too was absolutely covered in the muck as well. She removed her cloak and did the same. When the smell of rot was gone, she breathed deep.

"It will come back," Helesys said. "But we will not!"

She and Taunauk made their way down the passage, Taunauk leading and Helesys kindling her light at his back. The cavern stretched on, meandering only slightly, and shrinking the entire time.

They walked another mile before the tunnel was only six feet tall and just as wide. Both weaver and barbarian stooped and walked a little farther before it became clear the process would continue.

"Wait," Helesys said and stepped to the front. "Shield your eyes."

She stooped down again and flared her light as bright as she could. The passage stretched off into the distance, but at the furthest reaches, Helesys saw tunnels branching off of the main passage.

"Something was down there," Helesys mumbled. "But the tunnels grow ever smaller…"

"We could crawl a little further," Taunauk mumbled.

Helesys flared her light again and then bolstered her voice. *"We have spoken of dreams and entered this forgotten place. We have followed the path of Shéslang the Serpent seeking aid or guidance…"* She spoke in the tongue of the serpent, then repeated the words in all the languages they had encountered so far: The old words of magic, the language of the druids, and the tongue of the cannibals, but nothing answered. Only silence followed.

She relaxed her gauntlet and let the light fade to a mere torch. The pull Helesys had felt, the direction that she was so certain of, was gone completely. She felt nothing in her wand-arm save for the somber kindling of power for her light. The weaver tried not to let dejection show on her face.

"Let us rest a while," Taunauk said. He was already sitting down, cross-legged, before she could protest.

Helesys slumped down the wall opposite her comrade. They were deep enough in the tunnel that the light from the main cavern was gone completely, and there were no glowing flowers here. Her wand-arm cast harsh shadows over the barbarian and, she imagined, over herself as well.

She glanced over, half-expecting to see Shawn beside her, and lit similarly in the light. She chuckled and told Taunauk this.

"How do you think Shawn's faring?" Helesys asked.

Taunauk shrugged. "The rogue is shrewd and moves with stealth. I imagine he's doing as well as we are, if not better."

Helesys nodded; she couldn't deny the rogue's skill. But then there were lingering deaths like the parasite that whole cities had succumbed to.

"We both spoke to the Voice on the beach…" Helesys said. "Maybe Shawn did too."

"It follows. Remember to ask him next time."

She nodded. "I wonder who's helping us. It stands to reason that the dungeon is a truly massive place—that we have not explored all of it nor met the being that spoke to us… But it must be something truly powerful to hide from the Wolf-King. Likely a god… Maybe it is the Gatekeeper. Do you remember the writings in the Wode? They spoke of *her* forest and the dungeon. Then when we asked Amadeus about her, the Wolf-King came for us. What if the Wolf-King holds her against his will? What if she's the one helping us? Of all beings, shouldn't the original ruler be so strong?"

Taunauk nodded along. "All sound, but we do not know. How do we know this being is on our side at all? Did you feel something?"

"No. My wand was silent. It gave no clues. What do you think?"

The barbarian shook his head. "I don't know what to think. I do not trust the Voice. I trust you, and I trust Shawn. A god will not see us as equals. We may even be expendable."

Helesys looked upon her comrade, her thoughts turning back to the caverns and the blue creatures. Remembering what it was like to see two Taunauks and being unsure which was which.

"I fear I have made a mistake," she said. "In the caverns, the blue creatures turned my memories against me. I could not tell which was you and which was the imitation. If I hadn't shared my memories with you, then I would've seen through the creature's ruse. Perhaps… Perhaps, when our memories return, we shouldn't share them with each other, lest they be used against us."

Taunauk shook his head quickly. "It is my wish to share them. You are my sister-at-arms and my friend. To have gone through such battle and death and to say less would be an insult. I… I have no one else. I do not wish to keep things from you."

Helesys nodded hesitantly. "Nor I." In truth, she felt the same, but the thought of the scarce memories she had being turned against her, was too horrible a thought to ignore.

Rustling from down the passageway interrupted their conversation. Both weaver and barbarian rose to their feet, ready. Helesys flared her light.

A snake slithered along the ceiling of the passage. Its face was broad and flat, with deep red eyes. The length of it was a mottled green, like the surface of an algae-covered pond. It moved toward them in lazy, sweeping curves.

Helesys dimmed the light of her wand-arm and the pair watched carefully as it approached. When it was twenty feet away, it slunk down to the floor of the passage. Closer now, Helesys saw that the serpent's body was only as big around as her wrist, but the length of it trailed off into the gloom—easily fifty feet.

"*No need to stand,*" the serpent said, in the language of Shéslang. Helesys's wand-arm hummed in translation. Despite its stature, the serpent's voice was a deep, resonating hiss that echoed the length of the passage. It spoke slowly. "*It takes me much longer to travel than it used to.*"

Helesys glanced at the walls of the passageway, then back to the way they came to the immense caverns, then again to the serpent.

"*It* is *I, Shéslang,*" the snake said. "*The serpent whose path you walked and climbed. I made the cavern. The people built a city and monuments in my wake. Your eyes do not deceive you.*"

Only then did her wand-arm begin to hum, quiet and faint—as if the wand itself did not recognize the serpent.

Though Taunauk could not understand the ancient tongue, the outlander sat. Though it seemed a sign of reverence, he kept his axe across his lap. Then the outlander began to glow, a molten, shimmering orange.

Helesys had seen Taunauk's power several times, and each seemed a different expression—like a gemstone from different angles.

*"You have diminished, Shéslang,"* Taunauk said, his voice overlapping with one other—a woman's. *"Don't gods normally grow in stature?"*

Shéslang hissed in steady laughter. *"My kind… We are born at the precipice of our power. Gargantuan, violent, feral. I bore through the rock and earth, carving miles of tunnels in less time than we've spoken—And already my power faded. I left it on the walls. The glowing plants are the legacy. The souls that tend them are the dead left in my wake.*

*"It took hours to carve this passage, then years to carve those at the other end. I was scarcely bigger than this when I remembered how to speak and think. It will be many more years before I am small enough to fit in your hand, and ten times longer before I perish."*

Helesys had knelt down beside Taunauk and regarded the serpent. The old lemurs had asked why Shéslang did not save the city from the parasite… its power was long gone before then. So she asked, "What will happen to you when you die? Will you become large and feral again?"

*"That is what* would *happen,"* Shéslang hissed. *"I have been reborn before and I remember little except for destruction. I would become a monster again."*

"But that's not what will happen now?" Helesys asked.

*"No,"* the serpent said. Shéslang stared at her with its deep red eyes and slowly its mouth began to split in an 'X'.

Helesys's eyes grew wide—the lines were faint and the 'X' was small, but it was unmistakable.

Taunauk whispered in his double voice, *"You're infected, but it does not have to be the end. The parasite has not taken hold yet."*

*"I let them infect me,"* Shéslang said. *"Half a dozen lives of carnage and destruction. I do not wish to begin the cycle again. I do not wish to become a monster again and spend a dozen lifetimes mourning."*

The weaver's stomach turned. "But you'll lose yourself completely. I've heard the song. There is no one but the parasite."

*"I've heard it too…"* The serpent trailed off, the 'X' in its face twitching slightly. *"I wish to be something else, something more—even if I do not know what that is."*

Taunauk and Helesys looked to each other. Though his eyes and face were covered with the orange glow, she saw regret mirrored on his face.

Helesys turned to the serpent. "We seek both the Wolf-King and Zhug. We can bring back treasures across the realms… Can you help us?"

Shéslang hissed long and quiet, something akin to a sigh. *"I have not heard of the Wolf-King in some time, and I have not met your like in some time either."*

When the serpent didn't continue, Helesys said, "We've heard of others that were blessed. Who were they? Can you tell us anything about them?"

*"They were three humans; tenacious and strong. Three brothers who could bring back treasure across death. They sought the Wolf-King… same as you. If the Wolf-King lives, then they must have failed."* The serpent bowed its head at the realization. *"The Wolf-King would not be foolish enough to let them live."*

"Will you help us?" Helesys asked quietly, undeterred. "We will not stop. We will not rest—"

*"I will help you,"* Shéslang said. Then the snake turned round and slithered back the way it came in a slow procession.

Helesys and Taunauk waited in respectful silence as the serpent slithered over its own coils. The barbarian's glow continued and cast shimmering light on the walls. Before long, the serpent returned, slithering over itself again—and Helesys realized that they still had not seen the end of the long god.

It held a spear in its mouth. It dropped the spear at the feet of the weaver and metal echoed through the passageway. *"A gar from my own back. I can give you no more. If you fail, I shall need something to offer the next that come in your stead."*

Helesys rose and picked up the spear, then stood and admired it. It was one single piece of metal, perfectly cylindrical, light, and strong. Its color was unlike anything she had ever seen; the surface was swirls of silver, like ink mixed with water. No wraps or grips adorned the staff, but the metal felt warm and sure in her hands. At the end, rather than a blade, the shaft merely tapered to a point.

*"The spear is made from a fallen star. In the hands of a normal mage, it would make a formidable conduit. You will work wonders with it."*

"A conduit?" she asked.

*"Magic does not normally manifest in the physical plane. Conduits— magic items—are bridges from the realm of magic to the physical plane. The shield, the spear, your wand and arm, are conduits."*

Helesys followed Shéslang's gaze to her metal arm. "We still do not remember much. The arm's workings are a mystery to me, as are its origins."

Shéslang hissed quietly.

*"There is someone who can help you, weaver. If nothing else, they can unlock the properties of your arm."*

*"What of us?"* Taunauk asked quietly, many voices rippling over his own. *"What do you see?"*

*"I see shades and shadows. Faces. You speak as one but speak for many."* Again, the serpent hissed in contemplation. *"You seek answers. The seams of the world are weak here—I have made them so. Open the seam, and seek first the Cogheart—they live underground in a realm of storms. They will help you to understand the wand that lies in your metal arm. They will help you master the magic required to tear open the seams and walk between worlds at will, rather than by death.*

*"Then go to the realm of crystal and ice, seek the highest mountain—the Godpeak. Spirits and mortals commune there, and you, barbarian, will find better connection to the shades that live within you."*

Helesys turned to her comrade with steely resolve. "We shall find the Cogheart, then find answers at the highest mountain. Then we shall find Zhug and, with his help, reach The Machine of Antrikaumora."

Taunauk rose, the glow rippling across his body as he did. *"Together,"* he said.

With the Gar of Shéslang in her left hand, Helesys closed her eyes and held out her gauntlet—reaching for the invisible seams that ran between worlds. She felt a broken tapestry running throughout the cavern. The serpent's titanic rampage had not just bore through the earth, it had torn at the very seams that held the realms of the dungeon together.

The seams here were tenuous. Even more so than those in the Apothecary's realm. Helesys marveled at the power of Shéslang—to have done in moments what the Apothecary had spent lifetimes building.

Again she felt the slightest view of the realms that lay beyond sulfur and ash, creamy pastel paints, blinding bright light, a cacophony of screams, and then hair-raising static and the smell of rain—this she grasped.

Helesys held fast the seam that led to the Cogheart and bid it to open. *"Amplificare potentia!"*

The rippling of the seam grew to a pulse, the bubble to a boil. The crackle of thunder and patter of rain sounded through the cavern.

Helesys looked to Shéslang one last time. "Thank you. May you find peace."

*"May you find the answers you long for,"* the serpent replied.

Then the weaver reached for Taunauk's hand. The orange light faded from his skin and he alone took her hand.

~

Helesys and Taunauk stepped through the ethereal seam and into the familiar starting room of the dungeon.

There was always a bit of reluctance waking in that room. The thought of fighting through yet another realm always seemed a monstrous task. But this time both Helesys and Taunauk smiled wide.

At the edge of the room and the long hallway, stood a familiar rogue.

Shawn grinned and sighed heavily. "Took you long enough!"

~ ~ ~

NEXT TIME ON

*A BATTLEAXE AND*

*A METAL ARM*

Book 9:

*Ghost in the*

*Wheelhouse*

Available December 2021

# Spoiler–Free excerpt from *BAMA 9*

A mile later, the hallway ended on a rocky hillside made of black and jagged stone. The night sky above flickered with constant lightning and churned with stormwinds so loud they had to shout to be heard. The musky smell of rain lingered in the air.

"Which way?" Shawn called beside them.

Taunauk scanned the horizon, shrugged, and turned to Helesys. "I see nothing. What does your wand tell you?"

Helesys looked out over the blackened hills but focused on her gauntlet. There was faint direction… very faint compared to that which she felt in the caverns of Shéslang. If the latter had been stoic guidance, what she felt then was the meekest whisper. For the first time, it seemed as if her wand did not know which way to go.

The weaver pointed out over the jagged hills, following the faint direction.

"You don't seem certain," Shawn said.

"I'm not," the weaver replied, "but that's all we've got."

The heroes knew no peace as they crossed the hills. Their eyes scanned the blurred horizon where black storm met dark plains, and the hills were jagged rocks that could've belied smaller dangers. They moved cautiously over the uneven terrain. Helesys used the Gar of Shéslang as a walking stick and kindled strength to help with balance. They kept weapons at the ready and walked most of the way in silence, even though they saw no other souls.

At one point, Shawn said over the wind, "This is a wasteland if I ever saw one. Can we go back to the *Malorienta*?"

## To be continued December 2021

# Thank you for Reading

I hope you enjoyed reading this story as much as I enjoyed writing it.

If you did, I would massively appreciate a short review on Amazon or your favorite book website. Reviews are crucial for any author, and a starred review or even just a line or two can make a huge difference.

It's especially true for the start of a series. Thanks and I hope you enjoy the next one!

# Looking for more Engrossing Fantasy?

You might like ***Tales from Another World,*** an ongoing short story series containing stories about sorcerers, druids, mortals, gods, thieves, and all other manner of Terrans.

The $2^{nd}$ installment is out and it may or may not have ties to the world of *A Battleaxe and a Metal Arm*. So, if you're looking for more engrossing fantasy stories, read on and see how deep the rabbit hole goes.

# What questions do you have about *A Battleaxe and a Metal Arm*?

If you've read this far, hopefully you'll read a bit further—both in this book and across the series. I'm not sure how most authors write serials and how much of it is flying by the seat of their pants, but that's not how I do things. For all the major questions that might come up in BAMA, I already have answers for 95% of them. Same goes for the major plot points, twists and climaxes. That might sound boring to some, especially some of you other authors who enjoy variations of writing into the dark, but I think having a solid blueprint is paramount to writing a long series.

So, what questions do you have about the story? Here are a few:

1) ~~What is the dungeon?~~ It's a soul trap of overwhelming size and power. But where did it come from? Is it a force of nature or an ill-made weapon, or perhaps something else entirely?

2) Who were Helesys and Taunauk before they got trapped? At this point, we know little more than their names and abilities.  How well did they know each other beforehand?

3) How did Helesys get her metal arm? Likely through injury, amputation, and replacement.

4) Who is Shawn? Why does he feel so familiar to Helesys and Taunauk? The group speculates that they were traveling together for unknown reasons.

5) Who is the Wolf King and what sinister plans does he have for our heroes? How did he come to rule over the Dungeon? How does the Gatekeeper factor into all this?

6) Who is the mysterious voice encountered on the white sandy shores of Meridian? Why do they seek the death of the Wolf-King? …And why did they choose the heroes?

Did I miss any questions? Probably. Connect with me and other *BAMA* fans on social media and compare questions!

I've got plans. I've got answers. And I've got them on a drip-feed. Keep reading and expect to find out a little more to the mysteries with each installment. Hopefully, you're as excited about this series as I am.

# Connect with the Author

If you want to stay up to date on the latest about Samuel's publishing news and blog, check out his website and consider signing up for his monthly newsletter.

www.SamuelFlemingBooks.com

Samuel can also be found on Reddit, Goodreads and Facebook.

Samuel Fleming is a Science Fiction and Fantasy author.

He grew up in Maryland, spending most of his time swimming and writing. Swimming gave him a lot of time to daydream, so the two hobbies complemented each other well. Idle day dreams turned into stories, some of which stuck with him for years. These days he swims a little less and writes a lot more.

He loves a good story no matter the medium: Books, TV, video games, comics, tabletop RPG's, or podcasts–most of which he attempts to share with his wife and three kids, and occasionally on his blog.